How the Greedy Crane Was Killed by the Clever Crab

How the Greedy Crane Was Killed by the Clever Crab

TWO STORIES FROM THE PANCHATANTRA

Retold by

MEENA ARORA NAYAK

Illustrations by

Ajanta Guhathakurta

ALEPH

ALEPH

ALEPH BOOK COMPANY
An independent publishing firm
promoted by ***Rupa Publications India***

First published in India in 2024
by Aleph Book Company
7/16 Ansari Road, Daryaganj
New Delhi 110 002

This is a work of fiction. Names, characters, places, and incidents are either the product of the author's imagination or are used fictitiously and any resemblance to any actual persons, living or dead, events, or locales is entirely coincidental.

ISBN: 978-81-974969-7-4

1 3 5 7 9 10 8 6 4 2

Printed in India

The Tale of How the Greedy Crane Was Killed by the Clever Crab

In a verdant area watered by many streams, there was a large lake. In that lake lived an old crane, who was so decrepit that he could not catch fish any more to feed himself. One day, standing by the lake, feeble with hunger, he began to cry, his tears falling to the ground like a string of pearls. Seeing him in such distress, a crab, who lived in the lake, swam to the side and asked him: 'Uncle, why are you not catching fish today? Instead, you are standing here, quietly weeping. What's wrong?'

'You have correctly surmised my state of mind, nephew,' the crane replied. 'I've become extremely weary of killing fish to feed myself. In fact, I've decided to renounce food all together and give up my life. That's why I'm not attempting to catch even those fish that swim within my reach.'

'What is the reason for this apathy, dear uncle?'

'Nephew, I'm just saddened at the

thought of what will happen to this lake and the creatures that live in it. I was born near this lake, and my life has been sustained by it. Now I hear there will be a terrible famine that will last twelve years, and this lake will dry up.'

'Who told you this?' the crab asked worriedly.

'I heard it from astrologers. I heard that Shani will pierce Rohini nakshatra and collide with Mangal and Shukra. The result of this configuration is a twelve-year disaster. You see, when Surya's son, Shani, pierces Rohini nakshatra, Indra holds back his rain from earth for twelve years, and so the earth dries up and becomes barren, causing a famine that brings death to many. This lake of ours is already shallow, and I fear that lack of rain and the sun's scorching rays will dry it in no time. Can you imagine what'll happen to all the fish and other creatures who live in it? I've grown old with all these creatures. They are my companions. I've sported with them and celebrated with them. Their death will devastate me.

'In other lakes and ponds, creatures are already aware of this astrological event, and they're moving to larger waterbodies by themselves, or with the help of other creatures who are bigger and can transport them, such as crocodiles and porpoises. But the creatures in our lake are oblivious to the impending disaster. This makes me

cry, because I know they'll be wiped out, and I can't imagine life without them. That's why I've decided to just end my life by fasting till death.'

The crab was stunned to hear what the crane had to say. For a moment, he just stood there petrified, then he dived into the lake and hastily gathered as many of the inhabitants as he could to tell them what the crane had said. The other creatures, too, were struck by fear, thinking about the impending famine and devastation. Then, together they swam to the crane. 'Uncle,' they entreated, 'is there a way we can escape this calamity?'

'Yes, there is a way,' the crane replied. 'Very near here, there is a much bigger lake. Its waters are clear and sweet, and it is always covered with lotuses. It is so deep that even if the drought and famine last for twice its estimated time, it will not dry up. If you want to save your life, you should leave this lake and move to that one at once, by whatever means available to you. I, too, can help carry some of you to that lake.'

All the creatures quickly gathered around the crane, pleading, 'Take me! Take me!'

The cunning crane happily agreed. After that, every day, he took a few of the creatures on his back on the pretext of transporting them to the big lake, and, in a hilly area at a little distance, he smashed them on a rock to kill them and had a sumptuous meal. In this way, his days began to pass in the contentment that comes with a full belly.

One day, the crab came to the crane and pleaded with him: 'I was the first one with whom you shared the news; yet, you have been taking all the other creatures to safety, while I remain in this lake scared to death. Today, you must take me to the other lake and save my life.'

The crane had become a little bored with eating fish, and savouring crab meat for a change appealed to him very much. 'Come, nephew, I'll take you today,' he said and, putting the crab on his back,

flew to the rock which had become his feeding ground.

As the crane neared the rock, the crab started to see piles of bones on the ground. Fearfully, he wondered what place this was. 'Uncle, you must be tired from flying such a distance with me on your back,' he said to the crane. 'How far is this lake that you're taking me to?'

'There is no other lake, you fool,' the crane replied. 'Look down there. Do you see those bones? They belong to your companions. And this is what I intend to do with you, as well. I'll fling you on a rock, and you'll perish. Then I'll eat you.'

Terror gripped the crab, making him shake so much that he almost fell off the crane's back. He cursed the day he had listened to this crafty old crane and believed him.

Enemies become friends
and friends become enemies,
all to the purpose of one's
own gain.
Only the wise can discern
who is friend and who is foe.

Better to be in the company of
a snake
Better to invite a thief into
your home.
But shun an evil friend who is
two-faced.

Thinking these thoughts, the crab became

determined to destroy the crane.

When danger is impending,
fear it.
When you are face to face
with it
fight it with all your faculties.

Crawling up the crane's back, the crab extended his pincers and sank them into the crane's neck, slitting it from side to side till it tore right off. Then, carrying the severed head, he began to make his way back to the lake. It was a long and toilsome trip, but he didn't give up, and, as soon as, he gathered all the other creatures around him to tell them how the crane had lied to them and tricked them. 'There is no big lake,' he informed them. 'Nor is there an impending famine. It was all a ploy—an easy way for him to kill us and feed on us. After killing me, he would have returned to kill the rest of you, but I stopped him. Here is his head. Now we are all safe from that selfish, cruel, deceiving crane. Do not fear anymore.'

The Tale of the Fearful Rakshasa Vikala

In a city lived a king called Bhadrasena. He had a beautiful daughter who was replete with all good qualities. But a rakshasa had fallen in love with her and wanted to abduct her. Therefore, the king had his daughter protected with mantras and tantras so powerful that the rakshasa could not breach them.

However, he would visit her every night and just sit in one corner, watching her with lovelorn eyes. No one could see him, but his very presence made the princess tremble so uncontrollably, it was as though she was caught in a fever, and that is how her friends and attendants knew that the rakshasa was nearby. The rakshasa, however, did not know that his proximity affected the princess, or that she was aware of his presence in any way.

One day when the rakshasa came to the princess's room at midnight and sat down in a corner near her bed, the princess, feeling his presence, said to her attendant, 'That vikala (restless) rakshasa is here again. He comes every night and bothers me. I wish there was a way to get rid of him!'

The rakshasa heard the princess and thought that this 'Vikala' that she was referring to was another rakshasa who also visited her every night and was probably also prevented from touching her by the wall of mantras that protected her. 'I should see what this other rakshasa looks like,' he said to himself. 'Let me assume the form of a horse. That way he won't know who I am, and I'll be able to see him and assess his strength as a contender.'

And so the rakshasa changed himself into a horse and joined the other horses

in the royal stable. It so happened that that night a thief had also come into the stable to steal a horse. He looked at all the horses and chose the most handsome of them, which, of course, was the rakshasa in disguise. Saddling him quickly, the horse thief swung on to his back and rode away.

'This must be Vikala,' the rakshasa said to himself while he was being ridden strenuously. 'He has recognized me and probably wants to kill me. What should I do?' Just then, the thief whipped the horse, urging it to go faster, and the rakshasa's fear was confirmed.

After they had gone quite a distance, the thief pulled on the reins to stop the

horse, but the rakshasa kept galloping as fast as he could, trying to flee Vikala. The thief tried many times to halt the horse, but it seemed that the more he pulled on the reins, the faster the horse sped. 'This is not an ordinary horse,' the thief said to himself. 'Which horse does not stop when his reins are pulled? Is this a rakshasa in a horse's form?' Just the thought of that made him shudder in fright, and he began to look for a sandy bank where he could land safely after jumping off the horse. He was certain that if he remained on this rakshasa's back much longer, he would be killed—either he would fall off the speeding horse-rakshasa and break his neck, or the rakshasa would eat him when he stopped.

Then, to his relief, the thief saw a big bargad tree in the distance, and, as soon as the horse galloped under it, he grabbed a branch and climbed up into the tree. Thus, both the rakshasa and the thief were freed from each other, and they thanked the gods for their escape, feeling like they had received a new life.

On that bargad tree lived a monkey who was great friends with the rakshasa. Seeing his friend speeding away in the form of a horse, he called after him, 'O friend, why are you running away in such fear? This is a man whom you had on your back. He's your food. Why don't you just eat him?'

Hearing the monkey's words, the rakshasa stopped in his tracks, and changing himself back to his original form, retraced his steps.

When the thief heard the monkey call the rakshasa back, and he saw the fearsome rakshasa returning to the tree, he was so angry at the monkey that he grabbed his long tail and, putting it between his teeth, bit down hard on it. The monkey wanted to scream in pain, but he thought that this man was more dangerous than a rakshasa, so he restrained himself. However, his face looked so pained that when the rakshasa saw it, he couldn't help but exclaim, 'O monkey, the expression on your face clearly tells me that, like me, you, too, have been caught by the rakshasa, Vikala. Therefore, I think the best course for me is to leave as quickly as possible.' And the rakshasa ran away.